W9-AAA-609

THIS
BOOK
BELONGS
TO
DATE

PRESENTS

THE AMERICAN GIRLS COLLECTION

18 54

MEET KIRSTEN · An American Girl

KIRSTEN LEARNS A LESSON · A School Story

KIRSTEN'S SURPRISE · A Christmas Story

HAPPY BIRTHDAY, KIRSTEN! · A Springtime Story

KIRSTEN SAVES THE DAY · A Summer Story

CHANGES FOR KIRSTEN · A Winter Story

19 04

MEET SAMANTHA · An American Girl

SAMANTHA LEARNS A LESSON · A School Story

SAMANTHA'S SURPRISE · A Christmas Story

HAPPY BIRTHDAY, SAMANTHA! · A Springtime Story

SAMANTHA SAVES THE DAY · A Summer Story

CHANGES FOR SAMANTHA · A Winter Story

19 44

MEET MOLLY · An American Girl

MOLLY LEARNS A LESSON · A School Story

MOLLY'S SURPRISE · A Christmas Story

HAPPY BIRTHDAY, MOLLY! · A Springtime Story

MOLLY SAVES THE DAY · A Summer Story

CHANGES FOR MOLLY · A Winter Story

SAMANTHA SAVES THE DAY

A SUMMER STORY

BY VALERIE TRIPP

ILLUSTRATIONS ROBERT GRACE, N. NILES

VIGNETTES LUANN ROBERTS

PLEASANT COMPANY

For information address Pleasant Company, 7 North Pinckney Street,
Madison, Wisconsin 53703.
Printed in the United States of America
First Edition.

PICTURE CREDITS
The following individuals and organizations have generously given permission to reprint illustrations contained in "Looking Back:"
pp. 60-61—Edward B. Watson, *New York Then and Now,* (Dover Publications, Inc., New York, 1975); Courtesy Library of Congress; Harvey H. Kaiser, from *Great Camps of the Adirondacks;* Courtesy of The Adirondack Museum, Blue Mountain Lake, New York; pp. 62-63—Courtesy of The Adirondack Museum, Blue Mountain Lake, New York; Courtesy of The Adirondack Museum, Blue Mountain Lake, New York; Museum of Art, Rhode Island School of Design, Bequest of Isaac C. Bates; The Brooklyn Museum, 20.640, Museum Collection Fund; pp. 64-65—National Park Service; South Dakota State Historical Society; South Dakota State Historical Society; South Dakota State Historical Society.

Edited by Jeanne Thieme
Designed by Myland McRevey
Art Directed by Kathleen A. Brown

Library of Congress Cataloging-in-Publication Data

Tripp, Valerie, 1951-
Samantha saves the day: a summer story.

(American girls collection)
Summary: While spending the summer at Grandmary's summer home on Goose Lake, Samantha and her twin cousins decide to visit the island where Samantha's parents were drowned during a storm.
[1. Vacations—Fiction. 2. Islands—Fiction.]
I. Grace, R. (Robert), ill. II. Niles, Nancy, ill. III. Title. IV. Series.
PZ7.T7363Sam 1988 [Fic] 88-4943
ISBN 0-937295-40-X
ISBN 0-937295-41-8 (pbk.)

TO
CHARLOTTE KATHLEEN CAMPBELL
AND
PATRICK GRANGER CAMPBELL

Table of Contents

Samantha's Family

Grandmary

Samantha's grandmother, who wants her to be a young lady.

Admiral Archibald Beemis

A jolly Englishman who visits Grandmary every summer.

Samantha

An orphan who lives with her wealthy grandmother.

Uncle Gard

Samantha's favorite uncle, who calls her Sam.

Aunt Cornelia

An old-fashioned beauty who has new-fangled ideas.

. . . AND FRIENDS

HAWKINS
Grandmary's butler and driver, who is Samantha's friend.

JESSIE
Grandmary's seamstress, who "patches Samantha up."

MRS. HAWKINS
The cook, who always has a treat for Samantha.

AGNES & AGATHA
Samantha's newest friends, who are Cornelia's sisters.

ELSA
The maid, who is usually grumpy.

CHAPTER
ONE

PINEY POINT

TOO-OOT! With a cheerful blast of its whistle, the little steamboat chugged across Goose Lake toward Samantha. Its snappy red and white awning flapped in the breeze. Samantha skipped on her tiptoes at the end of the dock, waving both arms wildly to welcome the boat and its passengers.

"Yoo-hoo! Hello!" she called. "Agnes! Agatha! Hello!" As the boat came closer, Samantha could see Agnes and Agatha standing on the deck, waving hello to her. Their red curls were as bright as poppies in the sunshine. The twins were coming to stay at Piney Point, Grandmary's summer home in the mountains. Uncle Gard and Aunt Cornelia were with them. And so was Admiral Archibald Beemis. He came all the way from England every summer to visit Grandmary. Samantha danced with excitement. It was wonderful to have all of her favorite people together at her favorite place in the world. They would be just like a big happy family!

The boat pulled up to the dock, and Agnes and Agatha jumped ashore.

"Samantha!" they cried together. "Hello!" They swooped up to hug her. "We're finally here!"

"Agatha was seasick," announced Agnes.

"I was *not,*" protested Agatha.

"She was too," Agnes went on. "And we weren't even on the boat yet. We were on the sleeper train from Albany and . . ."

"Girls!" laughed Aunt Cornelia as she kissed Samantha hello. "Tell Samantha later. Right now you'd better scoot out of the way of the luggage."

The girls stepped back as the boatmen unloaded satchels and trunks, wicker baskets, and suitcases onto the dock. Uncle Gard and Admiral Beemis appeared behind the enormous pile of luggage. Uncle Gard was trying to carry two hatboxes, a parasol, and a picnic hamper. "Pardon

"Welcome ashore, Admiral," Samantha said.
"Grandmary will be so happy to see you."

me, miss," he said to Samantha. "Did I get off at the wrong stop? Is this Grand Central Station, New York?"

"No!" giggled Samantha. "It's Piney Point, Uncle Gard. Finally, finally everyone's here at Piney Point."

"Right-oh!" boomed the Admiral. He beamed with delight and saluted Samantha. His twinkly eyes were as blue as the lake.

Samantha saluted back with a grin. "Welcome ashore, Admiral," she said. "Grandmary will be so happy to see you. We've both been waiting all morning. Let's go up to the house."

Samantha led everyone up the steep hillside to the house. The twins exclaimed happily each step of the way.

"It's so cool here!"

"It smells like Christmas trees!"

"Oooh! Look! A log cabin! It's huge!"

Grandmary was standing on the shady porch of the big log house. She looked as cool and serene as a cloud in her white summer dress.

"Welcome to Piney Point, my dears," she said to the twins. "Gardner, Cornelia, hello!" She smiled as she held out her hand to the Admiral. "Archie! How lovely to see you!"

"Lovely indeed!" repeated the Admiral. "Mary, you look as lovely as the day I met you, more than thirty years ago." He bowed over her hand and kissed it.

Grandmary laughed, a little pink in the cheeks. "Oh, Archie, I am glad you're here. It doesn't seem like summer until you arrive."

"Summer it is," said Uncle Gard. "And I feel as boiled as a summer squash after that trip. Who's for a swim?"

"Me!" cried all the girls together.

"All right," said Uncle Gard. He was already loosening his tie. "I'll meet you at the lake in five minutes. Last one in is a rotten egg."

"Come on," Samantha said to the twins. "Let's go and change."

"Wait," said Agnes as she followed Samantha down the porch steps. "Where are we going? We don't have to live out in the woods, do we?"

Samantha grinned. "No. One of the best things

about Piney Point is that we all have our own little houses. The Admiral stays over the boathouse. Gard and Cornelia are in the Rose Cottage. And *this* is ours." She flung open the door to a one-room cottage. It had three tall windows facing the lake. Samantha had filled big baskets with goldenrod and black-eyed Susans. Their fresh woodsy scent filled the little house.

"Is this house for the three of us?" asked Agatha. "Just us and no grownups?"

"That's right," said Samantha. "Just us."

"I absolutely love it!" sighed Agnes. She flopped onto one of the three beds and looked around. "Look at that chair made out of tree branches. The branches are so shiny and twisted together, the chair looks like it's made out of pretzels."

"Our little house is like a treehouse," said Agatha as she leaned out a window into the waving branches of a pine tree. "Does it have a name, too?"

"Mmm hmm," answered Samantha. She was pulling her bathing suit over her head. "It's called

Wood Tick Inn."

"Wood *Tick?*" asked Agnes uncertainly. She sat up suddenly and looked into the corners of the room. "Ticks are bugs, aren't they? Is it called Wood Tick Inn because it's full of horrible bugs?"

"No!" laughed Samantha. "Not horrible bugs. But you *might* see a few ladybugs or spiders—"

"Spiders?" Agnes clutched her bathing suit to her chest.

"Oh, honestly, Agnes," said Agatha as she pulled off her long stockings. "You're not in the city now. This is the wilderness. There's *supposed* to be wildlife here. We'll probably see lots of bears and wolves and hear coyotes howling in the night. Isn't that right, Samantha?"

"Well, I've never seen any bears or wolves," said Samantha. "But there are lots of other animals to see, like deer and moose and rabbits. And the lake is full of fish."

"Do the fish bite?" asked Agnes.

"Of course not!" said Samantha. "Unless your toes look like worms! Come on! Let's go swimming!" She led the twins down a path covered with pine needles to the edge of the water.

"Look!" said Agatha. "Gard and the Admiral are out on that big rock in the lake. Let's swim to them."

"All right!" agreed Samantha.

"I think I'll just wade," said Agnes. She timidly put one toe in the water.

"I don't know what's the matter with her," said Agatha as she and Samantha splashed into the lake. "She's brave enough in the city, but here she acts like a scaredy-cat about little things like bugs and fish. Really!"

"Don't worry," said Samantha. "She'll get over it. Nobody stays fussy or scared at Piney Point. Come on! I'll race you to the rock."

❧

And Samantha was absolutely right. Piney Point quickly worked its magic on Agnes. In just a few days she was splashing straight into the lake, right along with the other girls. When the Admiral took them trout fishing, Agnes even put the worms on the hook with her own fingers.

Every day at Piney Point was filled with wonderful things to discover. In the morning Mrs.

Hawkins gave the girls sandwiches to put in their pack baskets and off they went exploring. Samantha showed Agnes and Agatha where sweet red raspberries grew on the hillside. She led them to a sunny meadow where they caught butterflies with their long-handled nets. The three girls canoed to the marsh. There turtles sunned themselves on the rocks, noisy birds nested in the cattails, and frogs poked just their eyes out of the water. One day they saw a mother deer and her fawn very near their house, and once they watched a big elk drinking out of the lake.

From early morning when the gauzy mist rose off the lake until late at night when lightning bugs twinkled all around them like falling stars, the girls were so happy and busy the long summer days just flew past. After two weeks at Piney Point, the twins' noses were sprinkled with freckles and their hair was golden orange. So the Admiral called them "the Tiger Lilies."

The Admiral was one of the best parts of Piney Point. Each afternoon he joined Samantha, Agnes, and Agatha for a swim. He paddled along with his head raised out of the water, like a duck. Sometimes he invited the girls along when he took Grandmary out rowing in the moonlight. He gave Samantha a genuine bo's'n's whistle made of shiny brass and taught her how to blow signals like the sailors did. And he gave all three girls sailor hats which they proudly wore whenever they went boating on the lake.

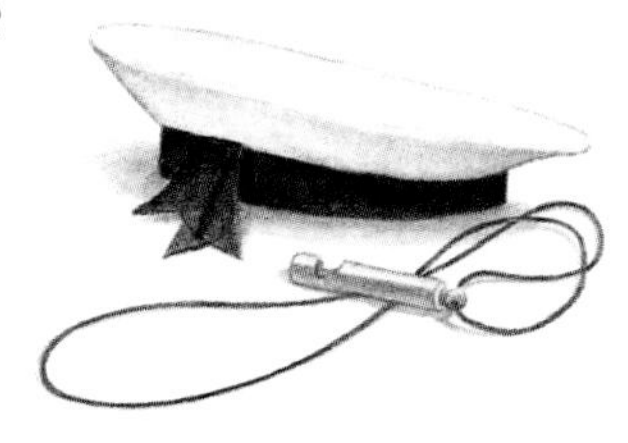

One hot, still day the girls were picking wildflowers on the rocky hill behind the main house. Samantha raced ahead of the twins and scrambled up to the top of a big boulder. She held an imaginary spyglass up to one eye and looked all around her. "Who am I?" she asked Agatha.

"You're Admiral Archibald Beemis!" Agatha cried. She climbed up on the boulder next to Samantha.

"Right-oh!" Samantha replied with a salute.

"Gosh," panted Agnes as she climbed up on the rock, too. "You can see all over from up here. You can really see why they call it Goose Lake. Over there is the goose's thin neck, and there's its head. That big island is its eye."

"Look at that pretty little island just below the goose's eye," said Agatha. "What's that called, Samantha?"

"That's Teardrop Island," Samantha answered. She climbed down from the boulder.

"Oh, because it's shaped like a teardrop," Agnes said.

"Do you see that rocky cliff?" asked Agatha. She pointed to a cliff at the end of Teardrop Island. "I'd love to climb that. I bet you can see all the way to New York from there."

"I have a great idea!" exclaimed Agnes. "Let's go to Teardrop Island tomorrow. We can go in the canoe and take a picnic and stay all day!"

"That would be fun," agreed Agatha. "We could bring our paints, too."

"No," said Samantha.

But the twins didn't hear her. "We can be real explorers," Agatha went on. "We can hike from one end of the island to the other."

"No," Samantha said again, louder. "I don't want to go there."

The twins were surprised. "Why not?"

"Because it's . . . it's not a good place," said

Samantha. She pushed her sweaty bangs off her forehead.

"But it looks so pretty," said Agatha. "What's the matter with it?"

"Are there bears and wolves on the island?" asked Agnes. "Is it dangerous?"

"The island isn't dangerous, but you have to go through that narrow part of the lake to get there," said Samantha. "It's filled with big sharp rocks."

"We can steer around those rocks," said Agatha. "That's easy!"

"The dangerous rocks are hidden underwater. You can't see them, but they can still rip out the bottom of your boat," said Samantha. She was quiet for a moment. Then she said softly, "That's where my mother and father drowned. There was a storm, and their boat was wrecked on the rocks. They were on their way back from Teardrop Island."

"Oh!" said both twins. They looked very sad.

"That's terrible, Samantha," said Agatha quietly. "That's just terrible."

"We're sorry," said Agnes. "We didn't know about . . . about what happened there. We didn't mean to make you feel bad, Samantha, really we didn't."

"I know," said Samantha. She bent down to pick some wildflowers growing near the boulder. "It's just that I hate to even think about Teardrop Island. It makes me sad, and scared, too. I never want to go there. Not *ever.*"

"I don't want to go there either," said Agatha.

"Me either," said Agnes. "Besides, there are plenty of other places we can go and things we can do."

"That's right!" agreed Agatha. "There are millions of things to do at Piney Point. Come on! Let's go swimming. It's too hot to pick any more flowers."

"We'll race you," said Agnes. She grabbed Samantha's hand. "Come on, Samantha!"

The three girls ran very fast down the hill toward the shining blue lake.

That night it was still very hot. The Admiral helped the girls drag their mattresses out to the little porch on Wood Tick Inn so they could sleep out in the soft, warm breeze from the lake. There was a patch of velvety black sky above them, framed by the tops of pine trees. Hundreds of stars glittered and winked at them.

The girls stretched out on their backs with their heads together. "There are lots more stars here than there are in the city," said Agnes.

"And they're much closer," said Agatha.

"Mmm," agreed Samantha.

The girls could hear waves lapping peacefully against the shore. The murmur of the adults' voices drifted up from the porch of the main house where Grandmary, Uncle Gard, Aunt Cornelia, and the Admiral sat to catch the breeze. Once in a while, the murmur turned into laughter. The girls could hear the Admiral's loud, hearty "Haw! Haw!"

Samantha smiled. "I love the way the Admiral laughs. He sounds like a happy donkey."

"He's the best grownup I've ever met," stated Agnes. "He's not afraid of anything. He's not bossy. And he knows interesting things. He knows more about this place than anyone."

"He's been coming here a long time," said Samantha. "He was my grandfather's best friend.

After Grandpa died, he kept coming anyway, all the way from England, every summer." She rolled over onto her stomach. "Can you keep a secret?" she whispered.

"Yes!" exclaimed the twins. They rolled over onto their stomachs, too, and wiggled up close to Samantha.

"Well," Samantha whispered, "I heard Mrs. Hawkins tell Elsa once that every summer the Admiral asks Grandmary to marry him."

"Gosh," breathed the twins, delighted with the secret.

"I guess Grandmary always says no," sighed Agatha. "I wonder why."

"Doesn't she like him?" asked Agnes.

"I don't know," said Samantha. "I think she likes him a lot."

"Well," said Agnes definitely, "if they ever did get married, you'd have a great grandfather."

"You mean a step-grandfather," corrected Agatha.

"I mean a grandfather who is great," said Agnes. "I think the Admiral would be the best grandfather in the world."

"So do I," said Samantha. She put her cheek down on her hands and closed her eyes. The soft breeze soon sang her to sleep.

CHAPTER
TWO

THE SKETCHBOOK

A dreary gray sky hung over the girls the next morning. During breakfast, it started to rain. The rain fell hard and heavy, swooping in sheets across the lake, ribboning down the windowpanes. By mid-morning the ground looked like soupy chocolate pudding.

Agnes moaned, "How can it rain so hard? The sky was perfectly clear last night."

"The weather can change very quickly here on these mountain lakes," said the Admiral. "Sunny one minute, rainy the next." He peered out the window. "We're in for it today. This is a real summer storm. Time to batten down the hatches! Foul weather ahead!"

The three girls just looked at him with faces as mopey as the moose over the mantel. "It's only eleven o'clock in the morning and we've already done absolutely everything there is to do," complained Samantha. It was true. They had helped Mrs. Hawkins make bread. They had been shooed out of Wood Tick Inn by a maid who wanted to dust. They had watched the boatman fix the big red canoe in the boathouse. They had pressed every wildflower they'd gathered the day before. Agatha had finished embroidering the tiny pillow she'd stuffed with pine needles from the evergreen trees. Samantha had rearranged all the postcards in her album. Agnes had worked on jigsaw puzzles for hours. The three girls had run out of indoor things to do.

"Well," said the Admiral cheerily, "since we can't go fishing we might as well play Old Maid, eh what?"

And so until lunchtime, the girls and the Admiral played game after game of Old Maid. The Admiral lost every game, mostly because he was so nice. "I say, Samantha," he'd exclaim. "I've just picked up the Old Maid." So everyone always knew when he had it in his hand.

After lunch the grownups all took naps. "How can they be tired when they haven't done anything all day?" Agatha wondered out loud. She plunked herself down on the bearskin rug in front of the fire.

"I'm bored," complained Agnes. "I wish we could go outside."

"I have an idea!" said Samantha. "Let's set up our easels and paint on the porch. That way we can be outdoors and not get wet."

"Good idea!" said Agatha. "I'm going to paint a picture of you, Samantha."

It was a little windy on the porch and rather damp, but it felt good to get out of the house. The three artists got out their wooden boxes filled with tubes of paint and worked happily and quietly for a while.

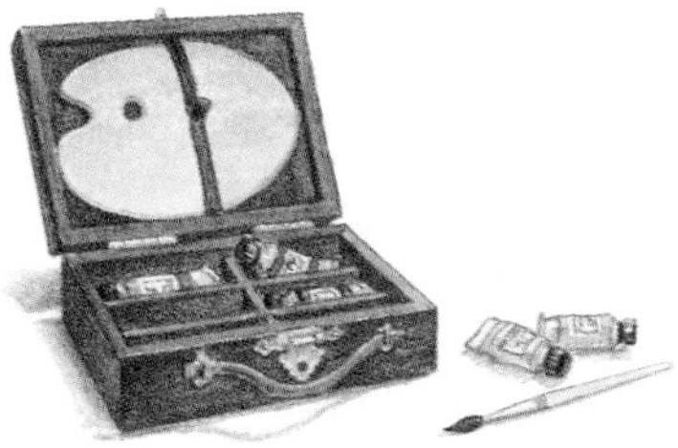

Then Agatha looked over at Agnes' easel. "Jeepers, Agnes," she said. "That's an awfully big rabbit you're painting."

"It's not a rabbit," said Agnes. "It's a sailboat."

"Oh," said Agatha. "How come it has ears?"

"Those aren't ears," said Agnes crossly. "That's supposed to be a flag." She sighed. "I have a little trouble making the paint go where I want it to go."

"I know what you mean," said Samantha. "This house I'm painting looks as if a giant had stepped on it and squooshed it."

The girls giggled.

"Maybe there's something wrong with these paintbrushes," said Agatha. She looked at the bristles of her brush. "Maybe they're worn out."

"Grandmary told me there are more brushes in the attic," said Samantha. "Let's go look for them."

Samantha led the way up the wide stairs to the second floor. They tiptoed past Grandmary's door so they wouldn't disturb her nap, and climbed up the narrow stairs to the attic.

The attic was long and dark. It smelled of dried flowers and dust.

"It's spooky up here," whispered Agnes. And it was, just a little. In the corners there were old chairs covered with sheets so they looked like lumpy ghosts. Outside, the wind swished through the treetops. The rain had calmed down to a steady soaking shower. It sounded unhurried, as if it would stay forever. The light from the windows was so murky, the girls couldn't tell what time of day it was, or even what season.

"Oooh, look!" cried Agatha. "Old hats! Boxes and boxes of them!" The girls threw off the dusty lids and lifted the hats out of tissue paper. The hats were old-fashioned and frilly. They had big floppy brims and wide satin ribbons. Agnes found one with a whole bird on top, and Samantha found one with an enormous pink bow. They put the hats on and paraded in front of a greenish mirror that sent back a wavery image.

They found gloves in another box, and beads, handbags, and shoes. In one box they found a stiff corset. Beneath a pile of old riding boots, Samantha found a box of photo albums and scrapbooks. The leather books were shut fast with brass clasps. Their gold-edged pages looked as if no one had turned them in a long, long time.

Samantha sat on the floor and opened one of the heavy books. The pictures were brown and yellow, and a little faded. Everyone looked very stiff and solemn.

"What is that?" asked Agatha. She sat down next to Samantha.

"It's one of Grandmary's old photograph albums," answered Samantha. "Jiminy! Here's a picture of Uncle Gard when he was little. Look at his long curls!"

"He's as roly-poly as a teddy bear," laughed Agatha.

"There he is with a fish he caught. That was taken right here, on the dock at Piney Point," said

Agnes. She was looking over Samantha's shoulder. "The fish is as big as he is!"

The girls fell into fits of giggles and sneezes from the dust.

"Is that you, Samantha?" asked Agnes, pointing to a dark-haired girl in one of the old pictures.

"No," said Samantha. "That must be my mother when she was a girl. See, it's labelled 'Lydia.'" She stared hard at the face that smiled at her from the picture.

"She looks just like you," said Agatha. "Her smile is the same as yours."

"Do you miss her and your father just awfully?" asked Agnes.

"I miss them, but I don't really remember them very much," said Samantha. "They died when I was only five." She sighed. "I wish I *could* remember more about them and the things we did together, but I really can't."

Agatha turned to the last photograph in the book. "Here's your mother again, with Grandmary. And that man must be your grandfather. Look at Gard, pretending to steer the boat!"

All three girls smiled at silly Uncle Gard.

"These pictures are funny," said Agnes. "I wonder why Grandmary keeps them hidden away up here."

"Maybe they make her sad," said Samantha. "Maybe they make her miss my mother and grandpa too much." She put the big book back in the box and pulled out a smaller maroon one. On the cover, it said "My Sketchbook." Inside, on the first page, someone had written "Happy Memories of Teardrop Island," and below that "Sketches and Watercolors by Lydia."

"What's this book?" asked Agatha. Her curls brushed Samantha's cheek as she leaned forward to look.

Samantha turned the pages slowly. "It looks like something my mother made," she said. "It's sketches and watercolors of Teardrop Island."

"She was a really good artist," said Agnes.

The girls were quiet as they looked through the book. There were tiny, perfect drawings of birds and squirrels, trees and butterflies. There were larger watercolor paintings, too. The colors were soft and shimmery, as if they came through

Samantha at the waterfall, 1897

the mist of a rainbow.

Near the middle of the book there was a picture that showed a little bare-legged girl standing in a shallow pool of water. She was holding on to a man's hands and smiling. Behind them was a tangle of wild roses and a beautiful waterfall tumbling down over mossy rocks. The sunlight poured through the trees, and its greenish light made the scene look like a fairyland. At the bottom of the picture it said, "Samantha at the waterfall, 1897."

"Oh, that's you!" breathed Agnes. "With your father!"

"Look at the waterfall," said Agatha. "Was it really that beautiful?"

"I don't know," said Samantha. She shook her head. "I don't remember anything about it. I didn't even know I'd ever been to Teardrop Island."

"But look," said Agnes. "The whole rest of the book is filled with pictures of you and your parents on Teardrop Island. You're having picnics and picking flowers. . . ." She flipped through the pages. "It seems like it was your favorite place. It looks

At the bottom of the picture it said, "Samantha at the Waterfall, 1897."

like your parents took you there lots of times."

Samantha stared and stared at the drawings. She had always thought Teardrop Island was a dark, sad place. But in her mother's drawings it was lovely and full of light. Teardrop Island didn't look like a place to be afraid of or a place to hate at all. Samantha turned back to the painting of the waterfall. She could almost smell the roses and feel the slippery, mossy stones under her feet. *My parents and I were together there,* she thought. *And we looked so happy!*

Suddenly she said, "Let's go there. Let's go to Teardrop Island."

Agnes and Agatha looked up at her. "But I thought you didn't want to go there, *ever,*" said Agatha.

"Well, I didn't know it was so beautiful," said Samantha. "And I didn't know I used to go there with my mother and father. I forgot. Maybe if I go back, I'll remember. I'll remember what it was like . . . and what my parents were like . . . and being together. . . ." She smoothed the page under her hand. "I just have to go there. Do you want to come with me?"

"Of course!" said both twins.

"We'll go tomorrow," said Samantha. "So we'll have all day. We'd better not tell anyone."

"All right," said Agnes.

"Look!" said Agatha. "It's stopped raining. Let's go out and splash in the puddles."

Samantha followed the twins out of the shadowy attic, down the stairs, and into the bright warm sunshine. She carried the sketchbook carefully in both hands. Now that she had found it, she never wanted to let it go.

CHAPTER
THREE

TEARDROP ISLAND

Samantha and the twins set out early the next day. Their pack baskets were jammed with sandwiches and cookies, butterfly nets, bird guides, and magnifying glasses—the same equipment they started out with every morning. But this morning, Samantha had her mother's sketchbook tucked away under the picnic blanket in her pack basket.

The Admiral came down to the dock to help the girls push off. "Where are you off to today, mateys?" he asked.

"Just exploring," answered Agnes lightly.

"Well, keep an eye on the weather," warned the Admiral. "It could turn nasty. That storm could

twist around and hit us again today. Anchors aweigh! Cheerio!"

"Cheerio!" the girls called back as their canoe glided into the deeper water. It was another hot day. The sun burned so strong it seemed to have bleached the sky white. "As soon as we get to the island, I'm going straight to the waterfall," announced Agnes. "It looks so cool in the pictures."

"I'm climbing right up to that rocky cliff at the end of the island," said Agatha. "I can't wait to see the view."

"I want to see *everything,*" said Samantha. She wondered what Teardrop Island would be like. Would it be just the way it was in her mother's pictures? Would she remember being there with her parents? Would it seem friendly and familiar, or scary and strange?

The lake was flat and peaceful. They paddled steadily, and soon Piney Point was out of sight.

"Watch it! Rocks ahead!" warned Agatha from the front of the canoe. The lake was suddenly narrow. Steep hills rose up on either side. Big boulders stuck up out of the water. Jagged rocks hid just below the surface. The water churned white where it splashed against the rocks.

The girls were quiet. They gripped their paddles and steered carefully. They had to zig and zag to find the best path around the sharp rocks.

"Go to the left!" Agatha would shout. Then, "Quick! To the right!" Samantha felt sweat from heat and fear dripping down her back. But the canoe was high in the water, so it slipped smoothly over the rocks beneath it. And it was so slender, it slithered between the boulders as easily as a fish.

Finally they were through the narrow passage and into a wider, deeper part of the lake.

"Phew!" said Samantha.

"We did it!" cheered Agatha, waving her paddle over her head.

"I bet even the Admiral couldn't have done better," boasted Agnes.

Now the canoe seemed to float by itself across the water into the cool shadow of Teardrop Island. As they came near the island, the girls could hear a chorus of birds singing gaily, as if the island itself were welcoming them. They saw a small stretch of pebbly shore where they could land the canoe. The rest of the shore was made up of big rocks.

As soon as the water was shallow enough, Agatha hopped out of the canoe and pulled the front end out of the water and up onto the pebbly shore. Samantha and Agnes quickly gathered up their pack baskets and climbed out, too. They were so excited they rushed up the steep shore, into the piney woods.

"We're here!" crowed Agnes. They threaded their way between the tall pine trees and moss-covered rocks. There seemed to be an old path, but it was so overgrown with giant ferns and long grass it was hard to tell. Overhead, leaves fluttered hello and squirrels leapt from tree to tree, inspecting their visitors.

"It's like a jungle!" exclaimed Agatha as she batted a branch away. "Now we're really explorers."

"It looks like the enchanted forest in *Sleeping Beauty,*" said Samantha. "As if it's been under a spell for a hundred years, just waiting for us to come."

The branches of the trees hung so low over the

path, it was like walking through a green tunnel. But once in a while, the girls would come into an open space between the trees where a surprise batch of wildflowers grew.

"I hear the waterfall!" cried Samantha. She ran ahead of the others to a sunny clearing. And there it was, looking just exactly the way it did in her mother's drawing: a lacy curtain of water splashing down giant steps of stones. The water spray caught the sun and made little rainbows. Samantha's heart thudded. It was the most beautiful thing she had ever seen.

Without a word, the three girls pulled off their shoes and stockings. They bunched up their skirts and waded into the shallow pool at the foot of the waterfall. They got as close to the fall as they could and let the spray mist their faces. The water was icy cold. It felt wonderful after their hot canoe ride.

"Next time we come we'll have to bring our bathing suits," said Agnes.

Samantha grinned. "I don't mind getting wet," she said. She pulled off her middy blouse and skirt and walked straight into the waterfall in her chemise and drawers. Agatha was right behind her.

And there it was, looking just exactly the way it did in her mother's painting.

"Ooooh!" they shrieked with glee as the water showered them. "Come on in, Agnes! It's *freezing!*"

Agnes took off her blouse and skirt, folded them carefully, and began to walk slowly into the pool. Then, "OOPS!" She slipped on a mossy stone and fell, plunk! on her bottom.

Samantha and Agatha laughed as they helped her stand up. "That's the fast way to get wet," Samantha giggled. She let the water pour down on her head and neck and shoulders until she couldn't stand the cold any longer. Then she ran out into the sunshine, then back into the falls again.

After a while the girls were cold down to their bones, so they stretched out on a warm rock to dry off. Samantha lay on her stomach and put her face into the water for a drink. "Oh!" she sputtered. "It's so cold it makes my nose numb!"

Agnes nodded. "My skin is all tingly," she said. "And I'm hungry. Let's have our picnic."

They spread the picnic blanket on the rock and sat cross-legged, holding their big sandwiches in both hands.

"This is the nicest place I've ever been in my whole life," said Agatha.

"It's so peaceful," said Agnes. "All you can hear are water, birds, and the breeze."

"Now that you've seen the waterfall, do you remember coming here with your mother and father?" Agatha asked Samantha.

Samantha kicked one leg in the water, sending sparkling drops into the air. "I think so," she said slowly. "I feel as if I've been here before, but it's all mixed up. It's almost like dreaming."

"Well, it's a dreamy place," said Agnes. She tilted her face up to the sun. Water drops hung in her hair like pearls.

"I'm very glad your mother drew those pictures," said Agatha. "Otherwise we'd never have come here."

Samantha looked around. It gave her goose bumps to think that she was in a place she had been with her mother and father, and nothing had changed. This very same rock and those very same trees were all in the pictures her mother had painted.

"Come on!" said Samantha. She stood up and brushed the crumbs off her lap. "Let's get dressed and explore. I want to find all the places my mother drew." She took her mother's sketchbook out of her pack basket.

"All right," agreed the twins.

Family picnic, Summer 1897

The sketchbook was like a treasure map. It led the girls on a long, happy hunt. First they found the grassy field where Samantha and her parents used to have picnics. It was just as sunny as it looked in the picture Samantha's mother had painted.

The girls looked a long time before they found the big split rock that was in another picture. They found flowers growing in the shade of graceful white birch trees. The same flowers were in the picture that showed Samantha and her father picking a bouquet.

Picking flowers with Father

And finally, the girls climbed up to the highest point of the island so they could see the view. The dark green pines and the hills that sloped down to the wide lake looked the same as they did in the pictures Samantha's mother had painted.

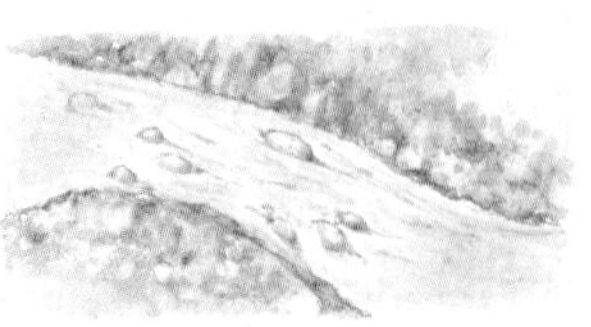

"Gosh! You can touch the clouds up here!" said Agatha.

"Look, there's the goose's neck," said Agnes. She pointed to the narrow rocky part of the lake they had paddled through that morning.

"And there's Piney Point," said Samantha. "It looks very small from here."

The girls were so high up they seemed to be standing where the sky met the land. The wind tugged at Samantha's skirt as if it wanted to lift her up like a kite into the clouds.

Samantha looked at the sky. The clouds were dark and heavy. "I think we'd better go," she said to the twins. "It looks like it might rain."

Agatha squinted up at the clouds. "You're right," she said with a sigh. "But I hate to leave."

"We can come back," said Agnes.

"Oh yes," agreed Samantha. "We can always come back, anytime we want to."

They hiked back to the waterfall, gathered up their belongings, and put their pack baskets on their backs. Samantha felt tired but content as they walked down the narrow path to the lake shore.

What a glorious day! She would remember it forever and ever. She was very glad they had come.

As the girls came to the edge of the water, the leaves of the silver maples were showing their shiny undersides. That was always a sign that a storm was coming.

"Is this where we left the canoe?" asked Agatha.

"I think so," said Samantha.

"Well, I don't see it," said Agatha.

"Uh oh," said Agnes. The girls stood in a row on the pebbly shore.

"Didn't you tie it up?" Agatha asked Agnes.

"No!" Agnes wailed. "I thought you did."

"Well," said Samantha calmly, "it's probably just drifted off a little bit. Let's walk around the shore and see if it's washed up somewhere else."

It was very hard to walk around the shore of the island. The girls had to climb up and down big jagged rocks that were slippery from the lake spray. Soon all three girls were wet and out of breath. The canoe was nowhere in sight.

"I'm cold," complained Agnes. "What will we do now?"

"Swim home?" Agatha suggested desperately.

Samantha wished she could laugh, but Agatha's silly ideas didn't seem very funny now. "We have to use our heads," she said. "Let's go back up to the rocky cliff. We can see all around the island from up there. We're sure to spot the canoe."

Wearily, they trudged up the same hill that they'd scampered up just a few hours earlier. They followed the path past the waterfall and up to the rocky cliff. By now the sky was the color of tarnished silver and the wind was strong. Samantha held her wet hair in one hand to keep it from blowing in her face. She looked all around, but there was no canoe to be seen. No canoe at all. Samantha's stomach flopped with fear.

"We're stranded!" moaned Agatha. "How will we ever get back to Piney Point?"

"Someone will come and get us," said Samantha.

"But how will they know we're here?" asked Agnes.

"We could send smoke signals," said Agatha.

"But we don't have matches. How can we start a fire?" asked Samantha.

"Uh, you rub two sticks together, I think," said Agatha uncertainly. "Or you can make paper catch fire with a magnifying glass. I read that in a book!" She pawed through her pack basket and dragged out her magnifying glass.

"It won't work. The sun's got to be shining," Samantha said. And the sun certainly was not shining at the moment. Big black clouds crowded next to each other, blocking the sun completely.

"Maybe if we made lots of noise someone would hear us," said Agnes.

So Samantha blew on her bo's'n's whistle as hard as she could. Agnes and Agatha shouted, "Help! Help! Somebody help!" But the wind was blowing so hard they knew no one could hear them. They gave up and looked longingly toward home.

"Jeepers, I'm hungry," said Agatha. "It must be dinnertime by now."

"Well, at least when we're not home for dinner they'll realize something is wrong," said Agnes. "In fact, they probably started looking for us when we weren't back to swim with the Admiral."

Samantha hoped Agnes was right. She sat down next to a big rock to get shelter from the wind. It was getting colder and colder. All three girls wrapped up together in the picnic blanket, but it didn't help much. It felt as if they sat there for hours, watching the sky get darker and darker. A chilling drizzle began to fall.

"We may have to sleep here tonight," said Agatha, hugging her knees to her chest.

Agnes shuddered. "I hope there are no wild animals to creep up on us."

Samantha started to say, "No, I don't think . . ." when they heard a rustling sound below them on the path.

"What's *that?*" Agatha cried.

"Shh!" hissed Agnes.

The girls heard more rustling. It might have been the wind, but it sounded more like a bear or a wolf pushing through the trees, coming closer and closer. Then they heard a moan!

Samantha gasped.

"Eeek!" yelped Agnes. She clutched Samantha's arm. The girls held their breath and listened. The sounds came closer: another moan, more rustling,

then a crash.

Samantha grabbed a big stick and stood up. "Get behind me," she whispered to Agnes and Agatha.

They heard the moan once more, and then a low voice struggling to be heard over the wind. "Help! Help me!"

Samantha lowered the stick. "Who's there?" she called.

"Help!" the voice called again. "Oh! Samantha, help!"

The girls looked at each other, then started

toward the voice, stumbling over one another as they headed down the hill. There, lying across the muddy path, was the Admiral!

"Admiral!" cried Samantha. She hurried toward him and knelt by his side. "What happened?"

The Admiral's voice was weak. "My head, my head . . ." he gasped. "I fell and hit it on the . . . on the . . . rocks." He put his hand up to his eye. In the darkness and rain, Samantha could just barely see the deep gash on his forehead and the blood that was trickling from it. The Admiral's eyelids drooped and he moaned again. "I came to . . . to help you," he whispered. "But now you'll have to help me." He tried to go on, but his voice failed, his eyes closed, and his head dropped onto the ground.

CHAPTER
FOUR

THROUGH THE PASSAGE

"Is he dead?" asked Agatha hoarsely.

"No!" said Samantha. "I think he's unconscious." The Admiral's eyes were still closed.

"What will we do now?" wailed Agnes.

Samantha didn't want the twins to see how afraid she really was. She tried to act as if she knew just what to do. "Well," she said, "the first thing we have to do is to make him comfortable. Let's get him over to that rock where we ate lunch. The trees will give us a little shelter from the rain. We'll have to drag him."

Agnes took one of the Admiral's arms, and Samantha took the other. Very slowly, pulling with all their strength, the girls moved the Admiral over to the flat rock by the pool. The Admiral groaned, but he did not open his eyes.

"He needs a doctor," said Samantha. "We've got to get him back to Piney Point as fast as we can."

"But how can we even get him to his boat?" asked Agnes. "He's too heavy to carry or drag all that way."

"We'll have to help him walk," said Samantha. She put her cold hand on the Admiral's forehead, then she shook his shoulder. "Admiral? Admiral, can you hear me?"

Slowly, he opened his eyes. Samantha and the twins gently helped him sit up. Then Samantha put one of his arms over her shoulder. Agnes took his other arm, and together they lifted him so that he was standing. He swayed for a moment, but then he steadied himself.

"Lean on us, Admiral," said Samantha. "We're going down to the boat."

The Admiral didn't say anything, but Samantha heard him take a deep breath. He tried to stand up straighter. His arm was heavy on Samantha's shoulder. Agatha gathered up all the pack baskets and led the way down to the shore. Agnes and Samantha struggled behind her, holding on to the Admiral's waist to steady him. The narrow path was slippery now because of the rain. Agnes and Samantha had to push wet branches out of the way with their free hands.

"That's it, that's good," Samantha murmured with every step. "You're doing fine, Admiral. Not much farther now."

The Admiral had left a lighted lantern in his boat. They headed toward it in the darkness. When they finally reached the boat, they helped the Admiral swing his legs over the side and lie down on the bottom. Samantha took a napkin from her pack basket, dipped it in the cold lake water, and laid it gently over the bloody cut on the Admiral's forehead. The girls covered him with their picnic blanket to help keep him warm.

"Girls . . ." the Admiral began. But his voice trailed off to nothing, and he closed his eyes again.

"All right," said Agatha in a wavery voice. "Let's go."

The three girls shoved the heavy rowboat into the water. The twins jumped in and sat side by side on the middle seat, each one taking an oar. Samantha knelt in the front, holding the lantern to light the way through the rain.

The Admiral's boat was much bigger and harder to handle than the canoe. The twins had to struggle against the wind and the choppy waves that slapped the sides of the boat. But they rowed slowly and steadily until they came to the narrow part of the lake where the rocks broke through the water.

"It's too narrow to row in here!" exclaimed Agatha.

"Use your oars to push off from the rocks," shouted Samantha.

The bottom of the heavy old boat scraped against rocks that were hiding beneath the water. On either side, boulders poked up out of the water like dark monsters. "Push right!" cried Samantha. Then, "Right again. Hard!"

The boat rocked wildly from side to side, knocking against the boulders. Water splashed into the girls' faces and drenched their clothes.

"It was probably like this the night my parents drowned," Samantha said to herself.

It was probably like this the night my parents drowned, Samantha said to herself. She shivered. Behind her, the Admiral stirred and groaned. *We've got to get through this passage,* Samantha thought. *We've got to get the Admiral back to Piney Point as soon as we can.*

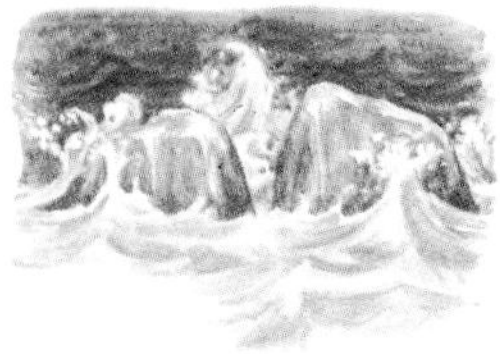

Suddenly, the boat stopped with a hard *thud.* "We're stuck!" Agnes wailed. The front of the boat was caught between two big rocks.

Samantha stood up and pushed against one of the rocks to get the boat free. She pushed so hard she lost her balance and almost toppled out into the water. She steadied herself, pushed again, and finally the boat was free.

"Quick! Everybody push hard to the left," Samantha yelled. After one more push they were out of the narrow passage, headed into the wide black lake.

They had no time to catch their breath. The twins began to row again. They hunched over the oars, trying to keep the rain out of their eyes. They rowed as hard as they could, on and on through the stormy darkness, across the lake that seemed as huge and endless as the ocean.

"Lights!" Samantha shouted at last. "I see lights! It's Piney Point!"

The twins twisted around to look at the welcome sight. In the main house at Piney Point, every lamp was lit. There were lights on the dock, and lights bobbing in boats on the water.

"Grandmary! Uncle Gard!" Samantha yelled. "Help!" She waved the lantern back and forth and blew on her bo's'n's whistle again and again and again. Some of the lights seemed to be coming closer.

"I think they see us!" she called to the twins over her shoulder. "I think they're coming!" She waved the lantern over her head. "Over here! Over here!" she shouted.

Out of the dark, she heard Uncle Gard call, "Samantha!" And suddenly, there he was in another boat alongside of them. "Samantha!" he said again. "Catch this rope. Tie it to the front of your boat. I'm going to haul you in."

"Hurry, Uncle Gard," Samantha said. "We've got the Admiral

with us. He's hurt."

Uncle Gard tossed a heavy, wet rope to Samantha. She tied it to the front of the rowboat as well as she could. "All right," she called.

With a jolt and a thump, Uncle Gard's boat began to pull them toward Piney Point. The boats moved quickly, and in no time they were at the dock. In the jumble of voices and lights, Samantha didn't even know who lifted her out of the rowboat.

"Be careful!" she said as the men began to move the Admiral. "He's hurt. Watch his head." And then Grandmary was hugging her so hard she could barely breathe.

"Oh my dear," murmured Grandmary. She smoothed Samantha's hair away from her face. "Oh my dear. Thank God you're all right."

Together, Grandmary and Samantha climbed the steps up the hill. Samantha's legs were wobbly. She leaned against Grandmary and followed the path of lights to the main house. At last, she and the twins and the Admiral were all safe.

Later on, the three girls were sitting in front of the fire in the big room of the main house. Cornelia had given them all hot baths, rubbed them dry, and wrapped them in blankets. They sat quietly, sipping their cocoa, watching the doctor take care of the Admiral.

"You're a lucky fellow, Admiral," said the doctor. He wrapped a clean white bandage around the Admiral's forehead. "It's a good thing these girls got you home so quickly. This cut could have been very serious. How did it happen?"

"Well," said the Admiral, "when I saw the storm coming up, I set out to find the girls. They weren't on the lake nearby, so I knew they'd gone through the passage. I had a bit of a time getting past those rocks in the rowboat. . . ."

"Oh, the rocks in that passage are terrible!" said Grandmary. "Especially in a storm!" Her face was pale.

The Admiral squeezed her hand to comfort her, then went on. "Once I was through, I heard your whistle, Samantha. Then I saw your canoe. It was partly sunk in the water near Teardrop Island. I suppose you didn't beach it properly."

The girls hung their heads.

"I realized you were stranded on the island, so I hurried to help you. I landed my boat and jumped out, but I slipped on the rocks and hit my head. After that, I don't remember much. I think I tried to find you. The next thing I knew, you were helping me into the boat. And then we were home, safe and sound at Piney Point."

The Admiral sat up in his chair as if it were a throne and his bandage were a crown. "I'm proud to know you girls," he said. He patted Samantha on the hand. "You really saved the day, young lady."

Grandmary sighed. "I was so worried about you, *all* of you," she said. "I was so afraid. It was just like the night, that awful night. . . ." She shook her head.

Samantha had never seen her grandmother look so weary. "I'm sorry we frightened you, Grandmary," she said. "I didn't mean to. I just had to go to Teardrop Island. I had to see the waterfall."

"You remembered the waterfall?" Grandmary

The Admiral patted Samantha on the hand.
"You really saved the day, young lady."

asked. She looked surprised.

"No," answered Samantha. "I didn't remember it. I saw it in this book." She pulled the sketchbook out from the folds of her blanket.

"Lydia's sketchbook," said Uncle Gard softly. "I haven't seen that in years. Not since. . ." He didn't finish his sentence.

Samantha handed the book to Grandmary. "I didn't remember anything about Teardrop Island. I didn't know I had ever been there with my parents, until I saw this book," she said. "That's why I had to go there today. I wanted to see the waterfall and all the places on the island we used to go. I wanted to try to remember what it was like when we all went there together, as a family."

Grandmary stared down at the book in her lap. "You and your parents had many happy times on that island," she said. "You are right to try to remember."

"It all looks exactly the same, Grandmary," Samantha said. "Everything on the island is just as pretty as it is in my mother's drawings. It's a beautiful, happy place. I'd like to go back again." She looked up at Grandmary. "Maybe you'd like to come with me sometime."

"Perhaps I will," Grandmary said softly. "Perhaps I will."

A Peek Into the Past

AMERICA OUTDOORS IN 1904

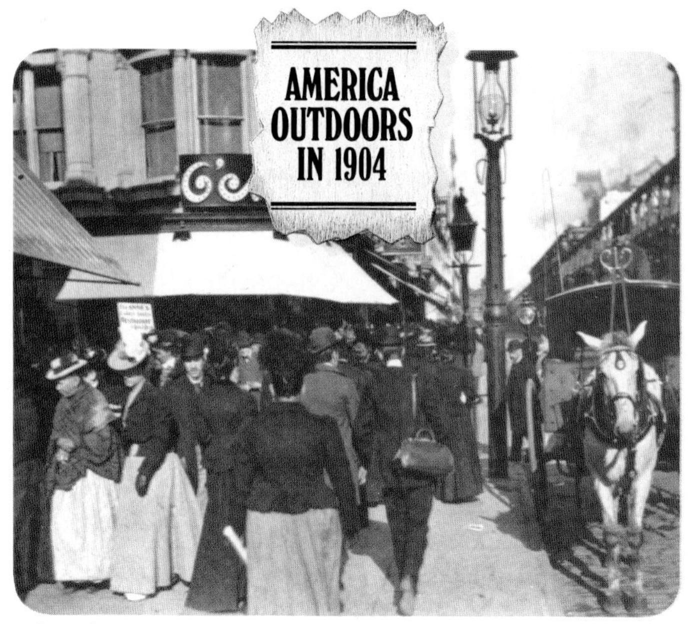

A busy shopping district in New York City

At the turn of the century, America's towns and cities were growing quickly. Families like Samantha's sometimes wanted to get away from crowds and noise and air that was gritty with coal soot. So in the summer they left their city homes for outdoor vacations in the mountains or at the seashore. Railroads made travel to vacation spots quick and easy.

Some families went to resort hotels and stayed for a week or two. Wealthy people like Grandmary often spent the entire summer at their own vacation *camps*. These camps were not like the summer camps some children go to today. Instead, they were large summer homes, often on private mountain lakes. There the outdoor air was clean and fresh. The scenery was beautiful. And vacationers could pretend they were *roughing it,* like pioneers in the wilderness.

Roughing it on vacation was very different from living like a real pioneer. A vacation home like Grandmary's was made of logs, but it was not a one-room cabin in the woods. It had a huge main lodge, several sleeping cabins for guests, and smaller cabins for servants, too. Sometimes all these buildings were joined by covered walkways. People used the walkways to go from place to place without ever really being outdoors. That was hardly roughing it! Furniture made from tree limbs made log vacation houses seem more *rustic.* Deer hoofs were

City people took trains to mountain camps like this one.

Wild animal heads and rustic furniture made vacationers feel they were roughing it.

used as hooks on walls, and antlers were made into chandeliers, too. Often elk and moose heads hung above fireplaces for decoration, and there were bear-skin rugs on the floor. Hunting, especially for large animals, was popular with men who wanted to carry on the traditions of rugged pioneers. But real pioneers had hunted for food. In 1904, hunting was a sport.

Although they pretended to live like pioneers in the wilderness, most vacationing American families led the same kind of lives in the woods as they did in their city homes. They traveled with servants who cleaned, cooked, and served them fancy meals. Vacationers packed huge trunks

In 1904, people dressed up even when relaxing outdoors.

Swimming and hiking costumes

and suitcases full of clothes so that they could always look just right. They read outdoor magazines and catalogues so that they would have the proper outfits and equipment for hiking, hunting, and fishing.

Even when they were roughing it, girls like Samantha were expected to wear dresses and long stockings—never shorts! They swam in very proper bathing costumes or itchy wool swimming suits. Women dressed just as they did in the city, changing from morning to afternoon dresses during the day and putting on fancy evening clothes for dinner.

Families like Samantha's loved their summer vacations and carried happy memories of outdoor days back to their city homes. They displayed collections of stones and shells they'd found, and hung photographs and paintings of outdoor scenes on their walls. They kept albums of pressed leaves and wildflowers.

Many people painted the vacation scenery.

They even made little pillows of pine needles to remind them of the spicy smell of forest air.

But some people realized it was important to save more than just memories of the outdoors. They saw that by 1904, most of America's frontier was gone. Railroads crisscrossed the country. The wilderness was disappearing and they wanted to save it.

John Muir worked hard to save America's forests. He started the Sierra Club, which you can still join today if you are interested in preserving the outdoors.

John Muir helped to save California's huge redwood trees.

Sarah and James Philip worked to protect buffalo herds.

Sarah and James Philip kept the buffaloes from becoming *extinct,* or dying out. Every buffalo alive in America today was probably descended from a herd they worked hard to save.

America's president in 1904, Theodore Roosevelt, added more land to our national forests than any president before or after him. Today you and your family can take a summer vacation in Yosemite National Park, look at towering redwood trees in Muir Woods, and still see buffalo because at the turn of the century, those Americans cared about saving the wilderness for us.

President Theodore Roosevelt in Yosemite National Park